B

Arranged by
John Stafford Smith

mf

O____say, can you see, by the

ly we hailed at the twi-light's last

through the per-il-ous fight O'er the

The
STAR-
SPANGLED
BANNER

The

STAR-SPANGLED BANNER

A Handbook of History & Etiquette

APPLEWOOD BOOKS

Carlisle, Massachusetts

Thank you for purchasing an Applewood book.
Applewood reprints America's lively classics—
books from the past that are still
of interest to modern readers.
For a free copy of our current catalog,
please write to: Applewood Books,
P.O. Box 27, Carlisle, MA 01741
or visit us at www.awb.com

ISBN: 978-1-55709-041-6

10 9 8 7 6 5 4

MANUFACTURED IN
THE UNITED STATES OF AMERICA
WITH AMERICAN-MADE MATERIALS

THE STAR-SPANGLED BANNER

★ ★ ★

Just decades after winning the American Revolution, in 1812, the United States found itself once again at war with Great Britain. In 1814, the British army over-ran Washington, D.C., setting the White House and Capitol building ablaze, looting the city, and forcing President James Madison to flee north to Maryland. The British followed, as demoralized American forces fled, and set their sights on delivering a knockout blow to America's third-largest city, Baltimore, Maryland.

At the time of the Battle of Baltimore, Francis Scott Key was a thirty-five-year-old lawyer and ama-teur poet living in Maryland. Great Britain had taken U.S. citizens as prisoners, one of whom was Doctor William Beanes. Key was asked to accompany U.S. government agent John S. Skinner to help secure the release of Dr. Beanes. They succeeded but were detained on the ship, as they knew of the British plan to attack Baltimore. From the British ship HMS *Tonnant,* Key witnessed the Battle of Baltimore. He saw the rockets' red glare and heard the bombs bursting in air during the twenty-five-hour bombardment. When it was over, he saw a massive American flag waving in victory.

Key wrote the first stanza of his poem on the back of a letter he had in his pocket. After returning to land, he wrote three additional stanzas at his hotel. Titling his poem "The Defence of Fort McHenry," Key coupled his poem with the melody of "The Anacreontic Song," composed by John Stafford Smith, which was the official song of eighteenth-century gentlemen's musical club the Anacreontic Society. It was then renamed "The Star-Spangled Banner."

COMPLETE VERSION OF "THE STAR-SPANGLED BANNER"

★ ★ ★

This version shows spelling and punctuation from Francis Scott Key's manuscript in the Maryland Historical Society collection.

O say, can you see, by the dawn's early light,
What so proudly we hailed at the twilight's last gleaming?
Whose broad stripes and bright stars, through the perilous
*   fight,*
O'er the ramparts we watched, were so gallantly streaming?
And the rocket's red glare, the bombs bursting in air,
Gave proof through the night that our flag was still there.
O say does that star spangled banner yet wave
O'er the land of the free, and the home of the brave?

On the shore dimly seen through the mists of the deep.
Where the foe's haughty host in dread silence reposes,
What is that which the breeze, o'er the towering steep,
As it fitfully blows, half conceals, half discloses?
Now it catches the gleam of the morning's first beam,
In full glory reflected now shines in the stream:

'Tis the Star-Spangled Banner! O long may it wave
O'er the land of the free and the home of the brave.

And where is that band who so vauntingly swore
That the havoc of war and the battle's confusion
A home and a country should leave us no more?
Their blood has washed out their foul footsteps' pollution.
No refuge could save the hireling and slave
From the terror of flight, or the gloom of the grave:
And the Star-Spangled Banner, in triumph doth wave
O'er the land of the free and the home of the brave.

O thus be it ever when freemen shall stand
Between their loved homes and the war's desolation!
Blest with vict'ry and peace, may the Heaven-rescued land
Praise the Power that hath made and preserved us a nation.
Then conquer we must when our cause it is just
And this be our motto: "In God is our Trust."
And the Star-Spangled Banner in triumph shall wave
O'er the land of the free and the home of the brave!

BECOMING THE
NATIONAL ANTHEM

★ ★ ★

The patriotic tune's popularity grew over the years. It was performed in taverns and included in songbooks throughout the country. It gained popularity during the Civil War. In 1861, American author Oliver Wendell Holmes added a fifth stanza, which was popular in the North, to reflect the country's current state:

When our land is illumined with liberty's smile,
If a foe from within strikes a blow at her glory,
Down, down with the traitor that tries to defile
The flag of the stars, and the page of her story!
By the millions unchained,
Who their birthright have gained
We will keep her bright blazon forever unstained;
And the star-spangled banner in triumph shall wave,
While the land of the free is the home of the brave.

In the late nineteenth century, the military started to use the song for ceremonial purposes. In 1917, the U.S. Army and Navy adopted the song as their anthem, though it wasn't until 1931 that "The Star-Spangled Banner" officially became the national anthem under President Herbert Hoover. Today, it is sung at military, sporting, and other events and is instilled in the memory of millions of Americans.

FAMOUS PERFORMANCES OF "THE STAR-SPANGLED BANNER"

★ ★ ★

YEAR	PERFORMER	OCCASION
1918	Fenway Brass Band	World Series
1957	Marian Anderson	Dwight D. Eisenhower's Inauguration
1961	Marian Anderson	John F. Kennedy's Inauguration
1965	U.S. Marine Band	Lyndon B. Johnson's Inauguration
1967	Universities of Arizona and Michigan's Marching Bands	First Super Bowl
1968	José Feliciano	World Series
1969	Jimi Hendrix	Woodstock
1982	Diana Ross	Super Bowl XVI
1983	Marvin Gaye	NBA All-Star Game

YEAR	PERFORMER	OCCASION
1984	U.S. Marine Band	Ronald Reagan's Inauguration
1984	Barry Manilow	Super Bowl XVIII
1985	Billy Joel	Super Bowl XIX
1987	Neil Diamond	Super Bowl XXI
1991	Whitney Houston	Super Bowl XXV
1997	Luther Vandross	Super Bowl XXXI
1999	Cher	Super Bowl XXXIII
2002	Mariah Carey	Super Bowl XXXVI
2005	U.S. Military Academy, U.S. Naval Academy, U.S. Air Force Academy, U.S. Coast Guard Academy Choirs	Super Bowl XXXIX
2012	Kelly Clarkson	Super Bowl XLVI
2013	Beyoncé	Barack Obama's Inauguration
2016	Lady Gaga	Super Bowl L

KEY'S
MANUSCRIPT

★ ★ ★

Key's manuscript can be found at the Maryland Historical Society. In 1933, the Wallers Art Gallery purchased the document for $26,400 at a New York auction. The gallery was in possession of the manuscript until 1953, when Mrs. Thomas C. Jenkins purchased the document, also for $26,400. She funded a carved marble niche to display the national treasure and donated it to the Maryland Historical Society.

THE STAR-SPANGLED BANNER THAT INSPIRED KEY

★ ★ ★

The flag that waved during the Battle of Baltimore was commissioned in 1813 by Major George Armistead, who was the commander of Fort McHenry. Flag maker Mary Pickersgill spent six to eight weeks creating the massive 30x42-foot flag with fifteen stars and fifteen stripes, one for each state that was part of the United States at the time. In 1918, the third Flag Act set the number of stripes to thirteen in honor of the thirteen original colonies.

THE STAR-SPANGLED
BANNER
AND THE SMITHSONIAN

★ ★ ★

Armistead was in possession of the flag at the time of his death in 1818. It was bequeathed to his daughter, Georgiana Armistead Appleton, who allowed it to be publicly exhibited at various events. Frequent requests were made for pieces of the flag, and the Armisteads gave fragments to veterans and certain other honored people. Georgiana said, "Had we given all that we have been importuned for little would be left to show." Indeed, although the family tried to limit the number of fragments given away, more than 200 square feet of the flag is missing, including one of the stars. Following her death, Armistead's grandson, Eben Appleton, inherited the flag. He lent it to the Smithsonian Institution in 1907 and bestowed it as a permanent gift in 1912, writing, "It is always such a satisfaction to me to feel that the flag is just where it is, in possession for all time of the very best custodian, where it is beautifully displayed and can be conveniently seen by so many people."

200TH ANNIVERSARY CELEBRATION

★ ★ ★

The 200th anniversary year for the "The Star-Spangled Banner" occurred in 2014, with various special events held throughout the United States. A particularly significant celebration occurred during the week of September 10–16, 2014, in and around Baltimore, Maryland. A new arrangement of the anthem, arranged by John Williams and with the participation of President Barack Obama, was performed on Defender's Day, September 12, 2014, at Fort McHenry. In addition, the anthem bicentennial featured a youth music celebration including the presentation of the National Anthem Bicentennial Youth Challenge Award to Noah Altshuler for the winning composition.

RESPECTING THE ANTHEM

★ ★ ★

While singing "The Star-Spangled Banner," certain protocol is followed. This is explained in United States Code 36 U.S.C. § 301:

(a) Designation.—The composition consisting of the words and music known as the Star-Spangled Banner is the national anthem.

(b) Conduct During Playing.—During a rendition of the national anthem—

(1) when the flag is displayed—

(A) individuals in uniform should give the military salute at the first note of the anthem and maintain that position until the last note;

(B) members of the Armed Forces and veterans who are present but not in uniform may render the military salute in the manner provided for individuals in uniform; and

(C) all other persons present should face the flag and stand at attention with their right hand over the heart, and men not in uniform, if applicable, should remove their headdress with their right hand and hold it at the left shoulder, the hand being over the heart; and (2) when the flag is not displayed, all present should face toward the music and act in the same manner they would if the flag were displayed.

AMENDMENTS

2008—Subsec. (b)(1)(A) to (C). Pub. L. 110–417 added subpars. (A) to (C) and struck out former subpars. (A) to (C) which read as follows:

"(A) all present except those in uniform should stand at attention facing the flag with the right hand over the heart;

"(B) men not in uniform should remove their headdress with their right hand and hold the headdress at the left shoulder, the hand being over the heart; and

"(C) individuals in uniform should give the military salute at the first note of the anthem and maintain that position until the last note; and"

"WHEN THE
WARRIOR RETURNS"

★ ★ ★

"The Defence of Fort McHenry" was not Key's first poem. "When the Warrior Returns" is another war-based patriotic ode written by Key after the Barbary War:

When the warrior returns, from the battle afar,
To the home and the country he nobly defended,
O! Warm be the welcome to gladden his ear,
And loud be the joy that his perils are ended:
In the full tide of song let his fame roll along,
To the feast-flowing board let us gratefully throng,
Where, mixed with the olive, the laurel shall wave,
And form a bright wreath for the brows of the brave.

Columbians! A band of your brothers behold,
Who claim the reward of your hearts' warm emotion,
When your cause, when your honor, urged onward the
    bold,
In vain frowned the desert, in vain raged the ocean:
To a far distant shore, to the battle's wild roar,

They rushed, your fair fame and your rights to secure:
Then, mixed with the olive, the laurel shall wave,
And form a bright wreath for the brows of the brave.

In the conflict resistless, each toil they endured,
'Till their foes fled dismayed from the war's desolation:
And pale beamed the Crescent, its splendor obscured
By the light of the Star Spangled flag of our nation.
Where each radiant star gleamed a meteor of war,
And the turbaned heads bowed to its terrible glare,
Now, mixed with the olive, the laurel shall wave,
And form a bright wreath for the brows of the brave.

Our fathers, who stand on the summit of fame,
Shall exultingly hear of their sons the proud story:
How their young bosoms glow'd with the patriot flame,
How they fought, how they fell, in the blaze of their glory.
How triumphant they rode o'er the wondering flood,
And stained the blue waters with infidel blood;
How, mixed with the olive, the laurel did wave,
And formed a bright wreath for the brows of the brave.

Then welcome the warrior returned from afar,
To the home and the country he nobly defended:
Let the thanks due to valor now gladden his ear,
And loud be the joy that his perils are ended.

In the full tide of song let his fame roll along,
To the feast-flowing board let us gratefully throng,
Where, mixed with the olive, the laurel shall wave,
And form a bright wreath for the brows of the brave.

FRANCIS SCOTT KEY

★ ★ ★

Francis Scott Key (August 1, 1779–January 11, 1843) was an American lawyer, author, and amateur poet from Frederick, Maryland, and later Washington, D.C. He was born to Ann Phoebe Penn Dagworthy (Charlton) and Captain John Ross Key at the family plantation, Terra Rubra, in what is now Carroll County, Maryland.

Key attended St. John's College in Annapolis, Maryland, graduating in 1796. He was a devout Episcopalian who considered becoming a priest, ultimately choosing instead to study and practice law under his uncle Philip Barton Key, a prominent lawyer who was loyal to the British Crown during the War of Independence. He married Mary Tayloe Lloyd on January 1, 1802.

Key became a leading real estate and trial attorney in Frederick, Maryland, and Washington, D.C. He assisted his uncle in the sensational conspiracy trial of Aaron Burr and the expulsion of Senator John Smith of Ohio. In 1808, he assisted President Thomas Jefferson's attorney general in *United States v. Peters*. Key assisted also in the prosecution of Tobias Watkins, U.S. Treasury auditor under former president John Quincy Adams, for allegedly misappropriating public funds. President Andrew Jackson nominated Key to be United States Attorney for the District of Columbia, a position he held from 1833 to 1841. In 1835 he prosecuted Richard Lawrence for his unsuccessful attempt to assassinate President Jackson at the Capitol.

Key had a complicated attitude toward slavery. He bought his first slave in 1800 or 1801 and in 1820 owned six slaves. By the 1830s, however, he had freed his slaves, and in the course of his career he represented pro bono several slaves seeking their freedom in court. Key was a founding member and leader of the American Colonization Society, the goal of which was to return freed African Americans to Africa. At the same time, he was associated with the American Bible Society from 1818 to his death and successfully opposed an abolitionist resolution presented to that group in the late 1830s.

On September 13, 1814, Key and British prisoner exchange agent Colonel John Stuart Skinner went aboard the HMS *Tonnant* to negotiate the release of American prisoners—among them Dr. William Beanes, who was cleared to leave because he had treated injuries in some British troops. The British did not allow the Americans off the ship until the next morning, however, because they had learned too much about British troop strength and locations and their plan to attack Baltimore that night. Key was unable to do anything but helplessly watch the bombarding of American Fort McHenry in what came to be known as the Battle of Baltimore.

As dawn broke, Key saw the American flag still waving: the Americans had held off the British attack and retained control of the fort. He was inspired to write a poem about his experience, which he completed over the next few days and which led eventually to the song we know as "The Star-Spangled Banner."

Key died on January 11, 1843, at age sixty-three. He was initially buried in Old Saint Paul's Cemetery, but in 1866 his body was moved to the family plot at Mount Olivet Cemetery in Frederick, Maryland. The Key Monument Association erected a memorial in 1898, where the remains of both Key and his wife lie in a crypt. Despite several efforts to preserve it, the Francis Scott Key residence was ultimately dismantled in 1947. Key was a distant cousin and the namesake of F. Scott Fitzgerald, and his direct descendants include geneticist Thomas Hunt Morgan, guitarist Dana Key, and American fashion designer and socialite Pauline de Rothschild.

ram-parts we watched,　　were so gal-la

glare,　　the bombs burst-ing in air,

flag was still there.　　O　say　do

wave　O'er　the　land　of　the　f